For Joni
love from Zeyde Mick – M.R.

For Alex and Niki – D.E.

BLOOMSBURY CHILDREN'S BOOKS
Bloomsbury Publishing Plc
50 Bedford Square, London, WC1B 3DP, UK
29 Earlsfort Terrace, Dublin 2, Ireland

BLOOMSBURY, BLOOMSBURY CHILDREN'S BOOKS and the Diana logo are trademarks of Bloomsbury Publishing Plc

First published in Great Britain by Bloomsbury Publishing Plc

Text copyright © 2023 Michael Rosen
Illustrations copyright © 2023 Daniel Egnéus

Michael Rosen and Daniel Egnéus have asserted their rights under the Copyright, Designs and Patents Act, 1988,
to be identified as Author and Illustrator of this work

A catalogue record for this book is available from the British Library

ISBN 978 1 4088 8329 7 (HB)   ISBN 978 1 4088 8330 3 (eBook)

1 3 5 7 9 10 8 6 4 2

Printed and bound in China by Leo Paper Products, Heshan, Guangdong

To find out more about our authors
and books visit
www.bloomsbury.com
and sign up for our newsletters

MIX
Paper | Supporting
responsible forestry
FSC® C020056
FSC
www.fsc.org

Michael Rosen

The Big Dreaming

Illustrated by

Daniel Egnéus

BLOOMSBURY
CHILDREN'S BOOKS

LONDON   OXFORD   NEW YORK   NEW DELHI   SYDNEY

Big Bear looked up at the sky and sniffed.
The Cold was coming, and it was time to get ready
for the Sleep – for bears sleep all winter long
and wake up in the spring.

Little Bear was worried.
"Will I **dream** during
the Sleep, Big Bear?"

"Oh yes," said Big Bear.
"You'll dream and dream
and dream."

"Is it," said Little Bear,
"a BIG Dreaming?"

"Yes, Little Bear.
It's a **Big Dreaming**."

Little Bear was still worried.

What if, what if, what if . . .

in the Big Sleep,

I run **out** of dreams?

Then there would be
a **Big Nothing,**
Little Bear thought.

I *know,* he thought.
I'll go and **look** for some dreams.

Little Bear wandered through the forest
until he met a squirrel.

"Squirrel, Squirrel, Squirrel," he said.
"We're getting ready for the Big Dreaming,
we're getting ready for the Sleep.

Do you have any spare dreams,

for when we sleep, deep, deep?"

Squirrel said,
"Yes, I had a dream.

I dreamed of **playing** all summer long
with my sisters. This is the dream of
Happiness Right Now."

"Thank you, Squirrel," said Little Bear.
And on he walked.

Little Bear wandered through
the forest until he met a rabbit.

"Rabbit, Rabbit, Rabbit," he said.
"We're getting ready for the Big Dreaming,
we're getting ready for the Sleep.

Do you have any spare dreams,
for when we sleep, deep, deep?"

Rabbit said, "Yes, I had a dream.
I had a dream that I was **lost**,
and I didn't know what to do.

But then a skylark flew past me.

And he showed me the path

all the way home.

This is the dream of
Coming Home Safe. "

"Thank you, Rabbit," said Little Bear.
And on he walked.

Little Bear wandered through the forest until he met a wolf.

"Wolf, Wolf, Wolf," he said.
"We're getting ready for the Big Dreaming,
we're getting ready for the Sleep.

Do you have any spare dreams,

for when we sleep, deep, deep?"

Wolf said, "Yes, I had a dream.

It was night and I was very young.

I was just a little wolf, looking up at the shining moon.

And as I looked, the light in the moon went out.

Like a candle blows out in the wind.

The night was darker than it had ever been,
and I was scared.

But . . .

. . . the next night, the moon
came back into the sky,
clear and bright and true.

Now I know that if the
moon disappears, it will
always come back.

This is the dream of
Always Having Hope."

"Thank you, Wolf,"
said Little Bear.

As Little Bear turned towards home, snow began to fall
from the sky, heavy and white. The Cold had come.
Oh no, thought Little Bear.
What if he didn't get home in time
for the **Big Dreaming**?

On and on he struggled, shivering
and lost and scared.

But then he remembered the dreams he had gathered.

Squirrel's dream warmed
him with **happiness.**

Rabbit's dream reminded him
of the **safe path home.**

And Wolf's dream told him
to **have hope,** always.

At last, he saw Big Bear's shape through the snow,
and he rushed towards it.

"You're back!" said Big Bear. "I was so worried!"

"Yes," said Little Bear, smiling.

"And I've brought back some dreams, so that we don't run out in the middle of the Sleep."

"That's good," said Big Bear, licking Little Bear's ear.

"That's very, very good."

"Big Dreaming, Little Bear," said Big Bear.
"Big Dreaming, Big Bear," said Little Bear,
curling up next to him.

And so, they slept.
And they dreamed . . .

. . . and dreamed,

and dreamed . . .

All the way to spring.